THE 7 CHARACTER STRENGTHS OF HIGHLY SUCCESSFUL STUDENTS™



# GRIT

RAMONA SIDDOWAY

rosen publishing's rosen central®

NEW YORK

Published in 2014 by The Rosen Publishing Group, Inc.
29 East 21st Street, New York, NY 10010



First Edition



**Library of Congress Cataloging-in-Publication Data**

Siddoway, Ramona.
Grit/by Ramona Siddoway.—1st ed.—New York: Rosen, c2014
p. cm.—(The 7 character strengths of highly successful students)
Includes bibliographical references and index.
ISBN: 978-1-4488-9540-3 (Library Binding)
ISBN: 978-1-4488-9559-5 (Paperback)
ISBN: 978-1-4488-9560-1 (6-Pack)
1. Work ethic—Juvenile literature. 2. Responsibility—Juvenile literature. 3. Self confidence in adolescence—United States. I. Title.
HQ796 .S53 2014
155.5'182

*Manufactured in the United States of America*

CPSIA Compliance Information: Batch #S13YA: For further information, contact Rosen Publishing, New York, New York, at 1-800-237-9932.

# CONTENTS

# INTRODUCTION

Kimberly Salmeri was born with two tumors known as lipomas wrapped around her spine. She had her first surgery at only ten months old. Despite several later surgeries, by the age of fourteen she had lost the use of her legs. Yet, through some incredible persistence, she somehow willed herself to walk. Mostly wheelchair-bound today, Kim has limited mobility and is able to walk a little, but only with intense physical therapy. But that doesn't slow her down. She decided that she would not let being confined to a wheelchair hinder her from helping others.

As a high school sophomore, Kim began raising money for CPL—Canine Partners for Life Organization. This group trains companion dogs to help individuals with disabilities lead a more independent life. For four years in a row she has raised thousands of dollars for the organization. Darlene Sullivan, executive director and founder of CPL, remarked that Kim has a huge heart and great leadership abilities.

"My struggles make me appreciate things that most people take for granted," says Kim. She really believes in

Kim Salmeri has demonstrated an astonishing amount of grit, resiliency, determination, and generosity not only in rising above her own struggles with illness and disability, but also in being so committed to helping others who face similar struggles.

people doing what they can to be self-reliant and independent, despite whatever disabilities they may have or adversities they may encounter. By focusing on helping others, she is able to face her own challenges in life. Kim is a person with true grit.

Grit means more than just perseverance. Grit is perseverance in the face of long odds, daunting obstacles, emotional or physical pain, exhaustion, and even isolation.

Grit is displaying resilience or persistence through adversity or discouragement. It is enduring a trying situation without complaint. It takes a firmness of character to have grit, to move toward a goal despite fear or failure. Some people call it "stick-to-it-iveness." Persistence is not necessarily a guarantee that a person will succeed, but any success is improbable without it. Most accomplishments and goals require a person to persist and "stick with it" for a certain period of time, whether it is for days, months, or years.

So why do some people seem to have more grit than others? Can grit be developed? Studies have shown that even just anticipating or believing in a positive outcome will promote and foster greater resilience and persistence. Conversely, having a poor attitude often decreases the reserve of grit that one can draw upon. Negativity and pessimism also increase the likelihood of quitting. The greater the positive mental attitude, the deeper and more sustaining the reserves of grit are.

Grit is a character trait that can certainly be developed, nurtured, improved, and strengthened. With training—and practice—people have shown marked improvements in their ability to persist and persevere even when faced with failure and setbacks. The following sections will discuss the different types of grit and how to develop and practice them.

# CHAPTER 1

# IT'S ALL UP TO YOU

Jordan Arbour fell out of a shopping cart at the age of three, resulting in extensive brain injuries. Jordan regressed and spent the next seven years relearning everything he had once known, including how to walk and talk. Normally brain injuries of this type leave a person permanently disabled and plagued by severe memory and coordination problems. In sixth grade, Jordan was still struggling to tie his shoes. It took a lot of determination from both Jordan and his mother to endure the many frustrations and setbacks of his years-long rehabilitation.

Things finally began to "click," however, and at age sixteen, Jordan sat down at the piano and, without any previous lessons, began to play Chopin's Opus 25 Ocean Etude. It was at that moment that Jordan decided he wanted to be a concert pianist. After a lot of grit that included finding a teacher who would be patient enough to teach him how to read music and deal with some slight lingering ticks from his accident, at age nineteen Jordan

The support and assistance of an entire community of gritty people are often needed in life—family, friends, and community members. This is known as "community resilience."

can now read music. He is enrolled as a music and math major at the University of Utah. His success is due in large part to the enormous amount of grit displayed by both him and his mother.

Jordan's story illustrates not only a personal and individual display of grit, but also that the support and assistance of an entire community of gritty people are often needed in life—family, friends, teachers, and community members. Community resilience is built upon the grit of individuals who come together to offer mutual support so that strength and resolve extend outward in wider and wider circles. A person who demonstrates grit can be an example to others and help those around him or her to tap into their own reserves of grit when struggling with adversity.

## THE MEANING OF GRIT

Grit is overcoming challenges and trials to achieve a goal. We sometimes call this trait perseverance, determination, or resilience. It is this character trait that makes it possible for an individual to stick to a task no matter how daunting the challenge or how high the obstacles that stand in the way. A gritty person keeps trying no matter how hard it gets, even when—or especially when—he or she faces failure, hardship, pain, exhaustion, fear, ridicule, or opposition. A gritty person realizes that bad times and setbacks are only temporary. Perhaps an old saying says it best: "When the going gets tough, the tough get going."

Grit is being stubborn in a good way, refusing to give up on or quit something because you know deep down that it is important to see it through to the end, whatever the short-term pain and personal cost. It means refusing to take no for an answer and refusing to be rejected or turned back.

Grit is refusing to give up or quit on something because you know, deep down, it is something important enough to see through to the end, whatever the short-term pain.

Showing grit is refusing to let anything stand between you and your goal, whatever that goal may be: getting a better grade, studying for a hard test, learning a new instrument, overcoming a difficult past, or even just becoming a better person. All of these goals take a lot of determination. Grit can make a person do things that he or she didn't previously think were possible.

## BEING AUTHENTIC

Some people think grit is an in-born trait. Conventional wisdom says that either you are naturally tough, resilient, and persevering, or you are not. While some people do seem to be genetically predisposed to grit, it is nevertheless a trait that can be cultivated, encouraged, and developed.

Part of becoming more determined is deciding what your goals should be and why. It is difficult to demonstrate a determination to persevere in something and keep moving toward a destination if you don't know exactly where you're going. Is the goal yours or your friend's goal, or is it copying a goal of a celebrity on TV? In the end, it will be impossible to demonstrate much grit if the goal you are pursuing is unworthy or isn't really your own. Having a determined, personally chosen, and authentic goal will increase the likelihood of urgently pursuing it. Any sustained adversity will divert you from a goal that is not closely held. It is very important to be true to yourself and surround yourself with supportive friends.

You don't want friends who are more interested in aimless distractions—and in distracting you—than in some worthy and important end goal.

Some people may be able to rely upon raw talent to achieve something, without having to dig deep to succeed. This is rare, however. The successful achievement of a goal typically requires confidence, determination, persistent effort, abundant energy, and lots and lots of grit. It can be easy to confuse inherent ability or raw talent with persistence and sustained effort. It is tempting to believe that grit and effort aren't as necessary when an individual is extremely talented in a given task. This person may be able to complete the task with minimal preparation, anxiety, and effort. Yet it is those who are considered merely ordinary or only modestly talented, but who display an extraordinary amount of toughness and determination, who demonstrate true grit.

Those who require only a minimal amount of grit to achieve a goal often become bored and tend to move on to other things. They often feel a sense of purposelessness and lack of focus and passion. But a person who has had to work harder for a goal will feel like he or she owns the goal or task. This person will be more likely to be persistent in achieving greater mastery over it or finishing it. Desire, or "really wanting it," will motivate a person to keep at it, and he or she will be more willing to put in the necessary time and effort to achieve

**Success requires sustained effort, persistence, confidence, and determination, even in the face of frustration and despair.**

that goal. This is especially true when someone really enjoys the task or feels it is an important part of his or her identity. You cannot be authentic in your goal unless you really want it.

Part of the trick is to somehow increase the sense of personal investment in the outcome. It is important to study and pursue your goal with determination.

So to begin, you need to know what your goals are, if they involve things that you are genuinely interested in and enjoy doing, and that they are chosen from both your heart and your head. It is very important to be on a path you love and surround yourself with people who will not abandon or judge you, people who will want to lift you up, not tear you down. Success—and the persistence necessary to achieve it—is achieved by people who feel excited about their goal, who feel that the particular goal or task is part of their identity.

## TEST YOUR GRIT

Ask yourself these questions:

1. Do I fail to finish what I begin?
2. Do I quit before I even start?
3. Do others say I give up too soon?
4. Do I lose my focus and get distracted when pursuing goals?

If some or all of your answers to these questions are yes, you may be in need of an injection of grittiness, STAT!

## IT IS UNDER YOUR CONTROL

Some people find they are not in a very supportive environment. They may be surrounded by negativity in their friendships, home, community, or school. It is hard to remain determined when a person comes from an abusive home, has teachers who don't work hard to help their students succeed, or has friends who are undermining or critical.

It can be a challenge to remain positive in a hostile environment. Distance yourself from negative people and look for people who support you and your goals.

Despite these and other obstacles, don't allow your surrounding environment to poison your determination in pursuit of your goals. This is a time when it is OK to be selfish. Choose inspiring positive images of the end goal to implant in your mind and continue to visualize them, especially when you feel most discouraged, exhausted, or hopeless. Distance yourself from those people who will try to undermine, mock, or break your determination. Look for those people who can and will support you. You can always find at least one.

Things will always happen that are out of our control—mistakes, accidents, setbacks—but they can be overcome. When a person feels personally responsible for a task or goal that he or she chooses for himself or herself, it is easier to persist.

The problem isn't always other people. Sometimes we put up our own barriers to success. This is usually done out of fear of failure, ridicule, or criticism. Failure is an uncomfortable and unpleasant feeling, as is opposition, criticism, or mockery. Part of grit is moving past those initial fearful feelings and overcoming the tendency to become so discouraged or intimidated that you quit. Failure and peer rejection can be a blow to one's self-esteem.

Part of overcoming this is to maintain a strong sense of self, a clear and unshakeable conviction that you like who you are, and you will not betray what you like about yourself to appease the underminers in your life. You should also realize that failure, setbacks, and negative treatment are not forever. They will pass. A little faith is required to keep moving forward with a positive image of success in the future.

Overcoming the temptation to quit also requires self-control and—believe it or not—a good mood! Studies have shown that when people are in a good mood, they persist longer on a task. Stay positive. It helps to locate the bulk of the blame for failure on low effort rather than low ability. Effort is under our control while abilities often are not.

This is where being authentic comes into play. Be excited about who and what YOU want to be and then go for it! When you are authentic, it's hard not to be psyched about your goals.

# CHAPTER 2

# EMOTIONAL GRIT

Bethany Hamilton's entire life was focused around surfing. It was her passion, and she assumed that she would continue the sport well into her golden years. So it was a shock that when Bethany was just thirteen years old, she lost her left arm to a shark while surfing. She was nervous that she would never be able to get up on a surfboard again. But she was also determined and gritty. Just a month after the shark attack, she was back in the ocean trying to surf again. After falling off the board the first two times, she became very frustrated. Her dad wanted to help, but Bethany insisted that this was something she needed to do on her own. She persisted, and on the third try she got on the board and rode all the way to the beach. She was thrilled! At age fifteen, Bethany went on to win the National Surfing Championship.

Bethany freely admits that she now has to overcome doubts and fears, whereas before the accident she had

Bethany Hamilton continues to be a highly competitive champion surfer despite having lost one arm to a shark while surfing. Her sheer grittiness allowed her to overcome any fears about getting back on her board.

been so confident, especially in the water. Every so often, when she surfs now, she feels a bit unsure. But she keeps pushing forward anyway, recognizing that every surfer has to face those same feelings at some point.

## FAILURE ISN'T THE END

Failure and loss are a necessary part of growth. Failure may feel absolutely awful, but it isn't something to be ashamed of. In fact, it can actually be good for you.

Setbacks and loss actually help develop deeper reserves of grit, especially when responding to pain with courage and determination.

By learning how to suffer setbacks and loss and still bounce back, we can actually become more resilient. We can develop deeper reserves of grit for use during future setbacks and trials. What matters most in living a life with grit is recognizing that it is not whether you win or lose, but how you fail, how you view that failure, and how you react to it and move forward.

Some people become very discouraged, even blaming themselves for their failure. But for those people who see failure as an opportunity or as encouragement to put in more effort, they actually build and strengthen new neural pathways in their brains. By changing views regarding failure, we can actually make our neurons grow. Carol Dweck, a Stanford University psychologist, says that new connections among synapses in the brain are formed every time something new is learned, and existing connections become stronger when learning is repeated. For this reason, failure is really the best teacher we have.

Emotional grit involves responding to life's challenges with courage, even when one is afraid. Resilient people move toward a goal through pain and grief by seeing that personal trauma and hard times are temporary. Some scientists suggest that pain, adversity, and even trauma may be necessary components in the process of finding happiness and fulfillment.

## STRETCHING WITHOUT SNAPPING

Another way to look at emotional grit is to think of a rubber band. When you pull the rubber band, the elastic stretches. Let go of one end and it bounces back. You can be like a rubber band. Whatever trial or bad time you go through, tell yourself you can bounce back just like elastic. Some trials may seem as if you are being stretched to your limits, and you feel like you are going to snap at any minute. But everyone is capable of grit. Just remind yourself, "I can do this!"

Learning how to "fail productively" by controlling emotions, adjusting thinking, recalibrating beliefs about ourselves, and adapting to change become essential elements in grit.

## MOVING PAST FAILURE

Bruce Pandolfini, the American chess master, teaches his students about perspective. Beginning chess players lose a lot. Those who go on to become better players learn to avoid past mistakes, adapt to the lessons that have been learned, control their emotions, and put the loss behind them. He teaches about seeing the "now" and comparing it with memories of the past. It is definitely OK—and often necessary—to go back and reinterpret past events and memories and use the lessons learned to move forward more effectively and successfully. By doing so, a person is able to find the strength and grit that was there all along. Most people are much more resilient and have more grit than they give themselves credit for.

Psychologist Edith Grotberg, Ph.D., suggests three things that every person should keep in mind and repeat to himself or herself: I have, I am, I can:

1) **I have**—Recognize the external supports that you have, such as strong relationships, rules, or even role models.
2) **I am**—Recognize the inner strengths that can be developed, the hope, compassion for others, and pride in self.
3) **I can**—Recognize the interpersonal and problem-solving skills that also enable communication and good relationships.

## FAILING BETTER

Is there a way to fail better? The magazine *Psychology Today* suggests several ways people can learn from failure and become more resilient:

1) **Lighten up**—Improve your sense of humor. Think about how that moment of failure today will make a great story tomorrow.

2) **Join the club**—You are not the only one who has failed in life. Find out how other people picked themselves back up and moved forward. Learn their techniques of grit.
3) **Guilt vs. shame**—Guilt focuses on what we did, while shame focuses on who we are. Recognize that you are a good person who just made a mistake. Look at the failure and learn from it.
4) **Optimism**—Focus on the positive and increase your flexibility in considering options and alternatives. Ignore negative thoughts, and you will increase your resiliency.
5) **Try volunteering**—By focusing on serving others, personal problems tend to shrink and become much more manageable and solvable. This allows more room and possibility for grit to flourish.
6) **Adjust personal expectations**—It may be necessary to revise a goal that you are repeatedly failing to reach.
7) **Journaling**—Writing helps create meaning, helps to sort things out, and helps with coping with failure. People who journal are less wrapped up in their past mistakes, are able to move beyond the sense of loss and failure, and are more optimistic.
8) **Beware of blame**—For a teen raised in an environment of domestic violence or abuse, self-blame can trigger or even worsen depression, which then

Journaling helps you to sort things out and move beyond mistakes, failures, and fears.

becomes an obstacle to resiliency. It is essential to recognize when some negative life circumstances are outside of one's control.

9) **Get moving!**—Try again or change course. Failure may be the best time to make the decision to try something different or new. Acting becomes the catalyst for grit.

# CHAPTER 3

# ACADEMIC GRIT

Luis Tinoco was the first male Latino to earn his high school's highest award, a full-ride scholarship from the University of the South in Sewanee, Tennessee. This seventeen-year-old graduate came from a single-parent home. According to one of his teachers, Luis earned a straight-A record through "sheer grit and determination." Luis did not have an easy life. At age nine, he had to finally stand up to his alcoholic father who then left the family. Luis used this paternal absence and bad example to motivate himself to excel and do better than his father did.

In sixth grade, Luis grew dissatisfied with the lack of progress he was making in the bilingual program, so he switched to all-English instruction. By the end of the year, he was making straight A's. As an entering high school freshman, Luis enrolled in AVID—Advancement Via Individual Determination. This is a national college readiness course that is designed to help underserved

Academic grit is sticking to a task despite difficulties, frustrations, or challenges.

students reach their highest potential. It achieves this through academic and social support and by holding participating students accountable to the highest standards.

The first in his family to attend college, Luis freely admits that he knows life is not fair and that it never will be. But rather than seeing this harsh reality as limiting, he instead sees it as a gift. Luis is not afraid to step out of his comfort zone. He always sees the value in others and is determined to make a positive impact upon the world.

## FLEXING THE BRAIN MUSCLE

Academic grit is displayed when a person is willing to persevere at academic tasks—homework, studying for tests, group work, regular class attendance. He or she sticks to it despite frustrations, difficulties, hardships, setbacks, or failures. The gritty person looks at academic achievement (or any achievement) as a marathon. A person with this kind of grit doesn't give up even when confronting such challenges as unsupportive peer cultures or neighborhoods where the interest in academics is limited or nonexistent.

So what if a student does not feel as if he or she was born smart, was not born into an academically or financially successful family, or lacks family or outside academic support? While family, school, and community are important factors in a student's life, the most important variable in the development and demonstration of resilience and grit is the individual. Even if the other three elements—intelligence, successful family, and academic support—are optimal, educational grit could not be present without the determination of the individual student.

Think of the brain as plastic. A student can actually become smarter—and more competent—when the brain is worked hard. It grows just like a muscle. When students become less afraid to fail, they succeed more. Trying—and failing—is what learning is all about. Analyzing one's failure and learning from it—rather than simply obsessing over it, while learning nothing and not moving forward—demonstrates true grit. It increases your capacity for perseverance in future trials, challenges, and struggles.

## GET OUT OF YOUR OWN WAY

Some students are so afraid of trying and failing that they do something to deliberately fail: they don't study, don't get enough sleep, create conflict with the teacher, or procrastinate.

A gritty person sticks with a goal and avoids distractions. It is the day-to-day follow-through that leads to success.

This self-sabotage offers a ready excuse for failure that doesn't call into question one's intelligence or ability. But when a student sets specific, detailed goals and meets them, self-confidence and experience with success will grow. This allows personal grit to increase as well.

Angela Duckworth, a psychologist who studies grit, comments, "The gritty person approaches achievement as a marathon. The gritty person sticks with it, whereas others might be distracted by boredom, failure, adversity, or plateaus." She remarks that a person would not progress in academics if he or she did not stick with a task to completion. It's easy to get sidetracked from one's goal when something potentially more exciting or easier to accomplish presents itself. A conscientious and gritty student will be organized, be responsible, follow through on academic obligations, and follow the rules. It is the day-to-day follow-through that leads to the ultimate success.

This truth is illustrated by Luis not only graduating from high school, but also doing so with honors. He decided on what really mattered to him—attending college. He had the discipline to avoid temptations and see it through to high school graduation. It would have been tempting for him to follow in his father's footsteps, to stay in an easier bilingual class, or to simply coast through school just to receive a basic diploma. But having grit means not settling for something just because it is easy or "good enough."

## TIMING IS EVERYTHING

It helps to win the mental battle before the tasks are even started. Something as simple as telling yourself to work for just fifteen minutes on a project or homework assignment can break through the mental block some students have. This modest commitment to a small period of work often creates a momentum that can keep you going until the assignment is finished.

Timing oneself can be a useful trick in maintaining focus. For example, when studying vocabulary, see how quickly you can memorize ten vocabulary words. Try to shift your focus away from potential distractions and toward the desired outcome and reward.

## KEEP YOUR EYE ON THE PRIZE

One mistake students make is trying to multitask, like switching between studying and watching television. This breaks focus and concentration. In any academic or learning area, focus and self-discipline are essential components of grit. An easier way to stay focused is to follow through on responsibilities immediately, like homework, school projects, or studying for a test. Immediately doesn't mean quickly or hastily, however. It means tackling your work and responsibilities before allowing yourself leisure activities and putting in as much time as necessary to get the job done well.

Acquiring skills takes hours of deliberate practice. It takes grit to resist distractions and temptations that may pull you away from your goals.

When working on a computer, avoid wasting valuable time switching over to surf the Web or check in with Facebook and other social networks. Don't be afraid to use tools to stay focused and motivated. Free programs such as SelfControl or Cold Turkey block distracting Web sites and mail servers for a predetermined amount of time. It's OK to need—and get—outside help to boost your grit.

World-class performers acquire their skills through thousands of hours of deliberate practice. Student who spend hours practicing—whether it be for chess, spelling bees, musical instruments, or studying—do so because they are interested in improving their performance. They do not do it because they always find these hours of study and practice fun or enjoyable.

When a person decides to engage in deliberate practice, he or she also decides to resist and avoid any distractions, temptations, or obstacles that may surface along the way. These can include parties, criticism from friends or peers who may mock the serious and studious person, lack of parental support, giving up when things get boring or difficult, watching television, texting with friends, etc.

Anything that disrupts focus from and dedication to an end goal is considered an obstacle. Studying in a room away from the television, computer, or refrigerator helps you avoid distractions and opportunities to procrastinate. Try turning the cell phone off for at least an hour.

# CHAPTER 4

# PHYSICAL GRIT

Holland Reynolds has been running long distance since the third grade. She ran the most important race of her life, however, when she was a junior in high school. It was to be a routine 3.1 mile (5 km) race for the San Francisco–area runner. But she had a cold, and the conditions were rainy and chilly. In addition, she was running with the knowledge that her beloved coach, Jim Tracy, was losing his battle against amyotrophic lateral sclerosis (ALS), or Lou Gehrig's disease, a devastating and terminal neurological disorder.

At about the 2.5 mile (4 km) mark, Reynolds was in third place and in good position to make her customary move to push ahead and win the race. Then something started to go wrong. Her legs weren't working properly. She began to hunch forward and weave off-balance. She was confused and disoriented. Given the cold and damp conditions, Reynolds had failed to hydrate properly.

Holland Reynolds shows her true grit in every race she runs, but never more so than when she willed herself to crawl across the finish line in a moving tribute to her ailing coach.

Despite his own difficulties with mobility, Coach Tracy found her on the course. He was shocked by her appearance but even more so by her grit. "Her vision was locked on her goal," he told the *New York Times*. "I'd never seen anything like it. It was like a mask of determination."

Reynolds stumbled on until she was just a few yards from the finish line, at which point she collapsed.

A race official asked her if she was OK and wanted to finish.If Reynolds didn't cross the finish line, she would be disqualified. Inspired by the grit Coach Tracy had shown during his battle with ALS, Reynolds said yes and slowly and agonizingly crawled the final few yards to cross the finish line. Afterward, she said, "All I knew was that I had to cross the line." Not only had Reynolds finished strong and honored her coach, she had also helped her team with the state championship.

## ENERGY, ATTITUDE, AND ZEST

Busy schedules and leisure activities like watching television, playing video games, listening to music, and using online social networking tend to crowd out many of the physical activities teens engaged in earlier in their lives. Even driving leads to a more sedentary lifestyle, as many teens no longer need to walk, bike, or skateboard to destinations. Yet physical grit and stamina need to be constantly exercised or they will be depleted and lost.

Physical stamina has a strong carryover effect regarding how a teen looks, feels, and performs in every area of his or her life. It even affects mental and emotional health. The more physical grit a teen practices and displays, the better he or she will be able to carry out daily activities with more energy, more zest, and a positive attitude. He or she will also be better able to stave off many chronic diseases. Physical health and endurance, and the grit they make possible, positively impact school and work life, social activities, personal fulfillment, and family life.

Physical endurance requires both mental and emotional stamina. With lifelong practice of physical stamina and endurance, paired with an equal helping of mental and emotional grit, a person is able to overcome many if not most obstacles. It adds to the ability to succeed in every other aspect of a person's life.

## I CAN SURVIVE THIS

Each of us has more resilience built into us than we realize. We have the capability to keep going through trials and challenges. Charles Horton broke his leg while skiing alone in the mountains. He was stranded for nine days before being rescued. Horton is quoted as saying, "This isn't fun but I can survive this . . . If you'd asked me if I could survive nine days, I'd have said no." But he did.

This type of grit and determination can be drawn upon and applied to any area of our lives. Whether the challenges are emotional, mental, academic, social, or physical in nature, there will be times in our lives when we will have to say, "This isn't fun, but I can survive this.

Keeping as physically fit as possible will help maintain grit and allows one to carry out the day with more energy, zest, and a positive attitude.

I can get through this and not only survive but succeed." Maintaining grit and keeping as physically fit as possible will be a benefit when we might be called upon to tap into those reserves, such as during an emotionally stressful time.

Not all obstacles are necessarily physical in nature. There may be a lack of parental support for your activities or a lack of adequate transportation to get you

# DEVELOPING COMMUNITY GRIT

It is not only individuals who can practice, develop, and demonstrate grit. Whole communities can as well. This is never more apparent than in the wake of natural disasters, when entire towns are devastated and suddenly sunk into chaos, confusion, and despair. Amid the wreckage and loss, individuals begin picking up the pieces. They begin banding together with neighbors to help each other out. Within hours, virtually all the townspeople are pulling together as one to heal and rebuild.

A particularly inspiring example of this is Joplin, Missouri. In the spring of 2011, a tornado packing 200 mph (322 kilometers/hour) winds tore through the town, killing 160 people, destroying thousands of homes, and severely damaging or destroying most of the district's schools. Yet a mere eighty-six days later, after a combination of rebuilding and repurposing of vacant buildings, the district's schools reopened, on time, on August 17. In the process, a sense of normality was restored, and healing had occurred.

Disaster relief and homeland security experts who witness and work alongside the victims of catastrophic events like the Joplin tornado or 2012's Hurricane Sandy that devastated coastal regions of New Jersey, New York, and Connecticut refer to the grit that is demonstrated during the recovery and rebuilding process as "community resilience." Such community grit is essential if a town or region is to bounce back from disaster. As with individuals, communities can build up and strengthen their reserves of grit and resilience. Some of the key factors to focus upon are developing a culture of self-reliance and independence; developing close-knit communities; identifying a leader and organization point for resiliency efforts; designing a robust recovery and redevelopment plan; speedy restoration of housing; and demonstrating early and highly visible evidence of recovery and rebuilding.

where you need to be in order to participate. You may doubt your abilities, be afraid to try something new, or be intimidated by outside influences trying to block your participation in a sport or other physical activity. A person may need to overcome a lack of willpower in becoming more physically fit.

Physical grit involves just as much mental stamina as anything, a belief that a goal is both attainable and worthwhile and that the endurance and discipline required to achieve it is realistic and available to you. Physical, mental, and emotional grit and fortitude are all interconnected. If you have them in abundance, they can feed and strengthen each other. If they are in short supply, what little there is can be drained away.

## THE SHORT AND THE LONG OF IT

Katie Ledecky is a fifteen-year-old 2012 Olympic gold medal winner of the 800-meter freestyle. In a *Washington Times* article, she was quoted as saying, "I just put in a lot of hard work this past year. Just progressively setting short-term and long-term goals. I've been dropping time progressively." Short- and long-term goals are essential to maintaining persistence in reaching any goal.

Katie had to take care of herself physically in order to persist in her freestyle goal. Physical grit was needed not only while swimming the 800-meter during the Olympics but also each and every time she practiced.

She needed to maintain a healthy body to succeed both in and out of the pool.

Persistence really just boils down to putting one foot in front of the other, repeatedly. It is the setting of a series of short-term goals that then lead in the direction of a long-term one. Often it's not until we have reached the long-term goal, turned around, and gazed back that we realize how far we've come, the distance we've covered, and the amount of grit that we contain within ourselves.

2012 Olympic gold medalist Katie Ledecky set short and long-term goals to win the 800-meter freestyle.

## THE RIPPLE EFFECT

Just by making a few small changes with your diet and exercise today, you can begin to increase your physical grit. You will also be more able to meet and overcome obstacles in other areas of your life. Grit and persistence are easier to summon when you have a healthy body.

Physical stamina, endurance, and grit play an important carryover role in almost every other area of a person's life. Being physically fit will help a person cope with school or social stress. A person with physical grit can contribute to community causes such as cancer awareness runs, disaster relief efforts, or Habitat for Humanity–style construction projects. Successfully enduring physical adversity and hardships will enable a person to achieve a more positive and optimistic attitude about life in general. The gritty person realizes that almost any obstacle can be overcome and any ordeal not only survived but triumphed over.

CHAPTER 5

# LIVING THE GRITTY LIFE

Taylor Howell is a typical fifteen-year-old sophomore who plays center on his junior varsity football team in Acton, California. Taylor, however, is blind. When he told his coach he wanted to play for the high school football team but couldn't because of his blindness, he was surprised by his coach's response. He said that Taylor would have to come up with a better excuse than that.

Diagnosed with cancer as a toddler, Taylor lost both of his eyes due to radiation and chemotherapy. Taylor has learned, however, that with grit nothing is impossible. His teammates on the football team don't cut him any slack. They help guide him to where he's suppose to be with physical or verbal cues. It might be a small tug on his football jersey or telling him outright where to move to stay correctly placed. Everyone agrees that Taylor is tough, sticking through two-hour practices every day and getting banged up at every practice. But Taylor persists. He plans on trying out for varsity and even wants to play college football.

Eric LeGrand was paralyzed while playing in a football game for Rutgers University. His determination and resolve have allowed him to, after much rehab work, regain movement in his shoulders and some feeling throughout his body. His grit was rewarded when he was offered an honorary contract with the Tampa Bay Buccaneers.

But for the short-term, he focuses on winning the next game, knowing that grit and persistence require taking things one step at a time.

## DIGGING DEEP IN THE GRIT

Grit or determination can be drawn upon to confront any challenge that may come up in your life. At home, a person may face divorce or death in the family, dysfunction, abuse, or lack of support. At school or in the community, there may be bullying or lack of educational or teacher support.

Think of positive strengths in your life—such as strong family support—and find ways to build on them. This can help build up greater reserves of grit.

Studies have shown that grit builds on itself. The more it is developed, practiced, and demonstrated, the stronger the ability to draw upon grit in future trials, struggles, and challenges. Think of the positive strengths in your life—personality strengths such as resilience or optimism; strong emotional, familial, or social supports that are already in place; innate and learned talents and abilities, etc. Now find ways to build upon them.

It helps to think of qualities that you already use or have used in the past when confronting a challenge or a problem. Think of a time when grit was used, even for a small task or a short amount of time. Use that memory as an anchor for a current obstacle that needs to be overcome. Those same qualities that were used in the past can be used now or in the future to overcome life's challenges.

## PUT "NOW" IN PERSPECTIVE

Sometimes a person may get caught up in the immediate problems or frustrations and forget the intended goal or the future reward. People often get stuck in the emotional trap that "now" will last forever. Disappointments are bound to occur, but gritty people avoid dwelling on or becoming paralyzed by them. They avoid turning bad experiences in their lives into catastrophes. Gritty people try to focus on a balanced view of life and avoid those extreme responses to adversity.

Resilient people recognize that life is comprised of both good and bad. Even if a situation seems riddled with strife, complication, and opposition, a resilient person will look at it with optimism and focus on the opportunities that are present. A blind football player may never see the ball but can still be part of the team and in the thick of the game.

Resilient people recognize that the bad doesn't last forever and focus on the opportunities that are present. Community resilience was on display in this neighborhood in the wake of Hurricane Sandy when neighbors came together to feed each other.

## IT'S ALL ABOUT ME!

Grit requires self-reliance, which involves a belief in oneself coupled with a realistic view of one's capabilities as well as limitations. Through experience and practice (lots of practice), confidence will increase and expand your abilities and reduce your limitations. Through meeting challenges successfully in life, a person will learn and refine important problem-solving skills, strengthen resilience, and increase adaptability.

# GRIT KIT

In what ways can you build up your capacity for and reserves of grit? Below are ten suggestions of what can go into your "Grit Kit" for current or future use at home, in school, in your community, or at work:

1) **STRIVE TO FORM POSITIVE RELATIONSHIPS THAT CAN BE A SUPPORT IN TIMES OF ADVERSITY OR WHEN PURSUING A GOAL.** Nourish current social support networks by supporting others in times when they need a shot of grit. People with quality social support are reported to have higher resiliency scores.

2) **AVOID PROCRASTINATION.** Stress always accompanies attempts to avoid challenges or crisis. Do not delay meeting challenges as they occur. Problems and obstacles do not go away by ignoring them. In fact, problems are usually compounded by not addressing them in a timely manner.

3) **FOCUS ON DEVELOPING BASIC LIFE SKILLS.** These include good decision-making, self-control, and maturity. These are all essential to grit.

4) **EXPECT UNCERTAINTY.** As our tolerance for the unplanned, unexpected, and unpredictable is increased, the anxieties that often accompany a need for certainty decrease. Less anxiety means greater capability for grit. It also allows for a more flexible, resilient, and adaptive approach to life.

5) **INCREASE YOUR SENSE OF HUMOR.** The ability to laugh at mistakes and setbacks becomes very freeing for a person. Humor also allows grit to thrive.

6) **BECOME INDEPENDENT.** This does not mean dissolving support systems but rather distancing oneself from unhealthy or unsupportive relationships, people, situations, or environments.

7) **BE SELF-MOTIVATED.** Grit involves a certain degree of internal initiative and motivation.

8) **FOCUS ON POSITIVE THINKING AND REVERSE NEGATIVE THINKING.** Thoughts are always translated into action, so focused, clear, and positive thoughts are essential components of a gritty personality and success in reaching goals and facing challenges.

9) **BE TOLERANT OF FRUSTRATION.** Facing challenges, trials, obstacles, adversity, and even boredom in the day-to-day process of achieving a long-term goal requires being able to handle the accompanying frustrations along the way, including setbacks and failures. Tolerating frustration along with developing emotional and mental flexibility are integral keys to grit.

10) **REMAIN BOTH OPTIMISTIC AND REALISTIC.** Expect a positive future and a successful resolution to challenges. A person may need to be flexible and realistic about what the definition of success in a certain situation may be. For Taylor Howell, for example, just snapping the football in the right direction needs to be in the checklist of his short-term goals. Don't punish yourself over failing to meet an unrealistic goal. Rather, set realistic goals, revel in your triumph, then immediately set a new goal that will force you to stretch further and push yourself harder. Remain optimistic that you will reach each successive goal, even if there are setbacks, delays, or unexpected obstacles. When you reach your goal, acknowledge how your positive attitude helped boost you over the roadblocks.

This is an important concept to internalize. In an emergency or when a crisis arises, people don't invent new behaviors; they instinctively fall back on what they've long practiced. Each moment, no matter how small, is a rehearsal for something larger, with higher stakes. In an emergency—whether it's facing a bully, dealing with a divorce or death in the family, or getting in an accident—you will need to call upon and display grit and resilience.

Get started on a "Grit Kit" by forming positive relationships with people who can be supportive when a quick shot of grit is needed.

Accepting responsibility for your own behavior and welfare and resisting the notion that you need to be rescued are great starting points for the development of true grit. Survival, persistence, overcoming adversity, and achievement of goals all involve an individual decision. They demand dedication to a process of self-improvement that requires hard work, lots of practice, and discipline. You must be ready and willing to try, fail, learn from failure, and try again.

Whatever amount of grit we have now, we can become even more resilient and determined in any area we choose. Being resilient improves every area of our lives—mental, physical, emotional, social, and academic. It protects against negative emotions such as depression, anxiety, and fear. It improves the quality of our lives. Find out where you are weak, strengthen those areas, and move forward with optimism and boldness. Anything and everything—including grit—gets easier with practice.

# GLOSSARY

**ADAPTABILITY** The ability to make or become suitable; to change to fit a new use or situation.

**COPING SKILL** A behavioral tool that may be used by individuals to offset or overcome disadvantages, disability, or obstacles, including the adversity of day-to-day life.

**DELIBERATE PRACTICE** The act of studying, memorizing, or practicing something while alone.

**DEPRESSION** A state of feeling sad or dejected, often accompanied by difficulty in thinking and concentration.

**DETERMINATION** Firm intent; an ability to be resolute.

**DEVASTATING** Causing severe shock, distress, or grief; overwhelming or stunning.

**FAILURE** An act or condition of not achieving a desired goal or falling short of a goal.

**FLEXIBILITY** The ability to change or bend; the ability to be versatile.

**GUILT** A feeling that you have done something wrong or bad or let someone down because of something you did or failed to do; wrongdoing.

**INDEPENDENCE** A condition in which a person is free from the control, domination, or determination of another person, power, or entity; relying on one's own ability; self-reliance.

**LOSS** A feeling of grief when something is gone or someone leaves; when something or someone is taken from you.

**NEURON** A nerve cell that transmits electrical signals.

**PERSEVERANCE** Persistence in sticking to a plan to reach a goal; continuous, patient effort.

**RESILIENCE** The ability to adjust to, recover from, or bounce back easily from a misfortune or unexpected change.

**SELF-ESTEEM** Confidence, satisfaction, and pride in oneself; a sense of one's personal worth.

**SELF-RELIANCE** Reliance on one's own abilities, efforts, resources, opinions, and decisions.

**SHAME** A feeling of inadequacy or sense of worthlessness due to perceived failure or falling short; a feeling of "I am no good."

**STAMINA** Strength or vigor; withstanding fatigue and overcoming resistance.

**ZEST** Liveliness or energy; gusto.

# FOR MORE INFORMATION

American Psychological Association (APA)
750 First Street NE
Washington, DC 20002-4242
(800) 374-2721 or (202) 336-5500
Web site: http://www.apa.org

The APA is the largest scientific and professional psychological organization in the United States. On its Web site are links to various topics and information, including dealing with anxiety, bullying, death, trauma, etc.

Association for Psychological Science (APS)
1133 15th Street NW, Suite 1000
Washington, DC 20005
(202) 293-9300
Web site: http://www.psychologicalscience.org

The APS is a nonprofit dedicated to the advancement of scientific psychology with a mandate to promote, protect, and advance the interests of scientifically oriented psychology in research, application, teaching, and the improvement of human welfare. The Web site has excellent articles dealing with many aspects of grit that can help further the reader's understanding and development of this character strength.

BAM! (Body and Mind)
Centers for Disease Control and Prevention (CDC)
1600 Clifton Road

Atlanta, GA 30333
(404) 639-3311
Web site: http://www.bam.gov
BAM! offers information and support about diseases, fitness, peer pressure, nutrition, and other topics relevant to the development and fostering of grit, resilience, and an emotionally and physically healthy person.

Boy Scouts of America (BSA)
P.O. Box 152079
Irving, TX 75015-2079
Web site: http://www.scouting.org
The BSA program builds character, trains youth in the responsibilities of participatory citizenship, and develops personal fitness.

Girl Scouts of the USA
420 Fifth Avenue
New York, NY 10018-2798
(800) GSUSA 4 U ([800] 478-7248)
Web site: http://www.girlscouts.org
The Girl Scout program provides experiences, field trips, community service projects, skill-building clinics, and other activities with a focus on developing values to guide actions and sound decision making. The program aims to build leadership skills, courage, confidence, and character.

GoodLife Kids Foundation
201 King Street
London, ON N6A 1C9
Canada
(519) 661-0190, ext. 273
Web site: http://www.goodlifekids.com

The GoodLife Kids Foundation strives to "inspire, support, and create opportunities to help kids live more active and healthy lives." The organization offers resources and programs across Canada. The Web site includes recipes and activities and provides grants to other organizations that offer sustainable physical activity programs for kids ages four to fourteen.

Junior Achievement
One Education Way
Colorado Springs, CO 80906
(719) 540-8000
Web site: http://www.ja.org

Junior Achievement is an organization that educates students in workforce readiness, entrepreneurship, and financial literacy through hands-on programs. Volunteers aim to inspire and empower students to believe in themselves, to make smart academic and economic choices, and to make a positive difference in the world.

Scouts Canada
1345 Baseline Road
Ottawa, ON K2C 0A7
Canada
(888) 855-3336
Web site: http://www.scouts.ca

Scouts Canada is a national organization that offers challenging programs for boys, girls, and youth ages five to twenty-six. Varying life skills are taught and learned, in addition to engaging in exciting and rewarding physical challenges and adventures.

## WEB SITES

Due to the changing nature of Internet links, Rosen Publishing has developed an online list of Web sites related to the subject of this book. This site is updated regularly. Please use this link to access the list:

http://www.rosenlinks.com/7CHAR/Grit

# FOR FURTHER READING

Brees, Drew. *Coming Back Stronger: Unleashing the Hidden Power of Adversity.* Carol Stream, IL: Tyndale House Publishers, 2011.

Catt, Michael, and Amy Parker. *Courageous Teens.* Nashville, TN: B&H Publishing Group, 2012.

Fox, Marci, Leslie Sokol, Aaron Beck, and Judith Beck. *Think Confident, Be Confident for Teens: A Cognitive Therapy Guide to Overcoming Self-Doubt and Creating Unshakable Self-Esteem* (Instant Help Solutions). Oakland, CA: New Harbinger Publications, 2011.

Gutwein, Austin, and Todd Hillard. *Take Your Best Shot: Do Something Bigger Than Yourself.* Nashville, TN: Thomas Nelson Press, 2009.

Lawrence, Marcia Pruchno. *Resilience: From Shavl to Southfield via Dachau.* Seattle, WA: CreateSpace, 2011.

Palmer, Libbi. *The PTSD Workbook for Teens: Simple, Effective Skills for Healing Trauma* (Instant Help Book for Teens). Oakland, CA: New Harbinger Publications, 2012.

# BIBLIOGRAPHY


Hafner, Katie. "Runner Crawls to Finish to Win Title for Her Ailing Coach." *New York Times*, December 1, 2010. Retrieved February 2013 (http://www.nytimes.com/2010/12/02/sports/02runner.html).

Bellenir, Karen, ed. *Fitness Information for Teens: Health Tips About Exercise, Physical Well-Being, and Health Maintenance.* Detroit, MI: Peter E. Ruffner, 2004.

Cannon, Ellen. "Joplin, Missouri's Victory: A Model of Resilience." Examiner.com, August 18, 2011. Retrieved January 2013 (http://www.examiner.com/article/joplin-missouri-s-victory-a-model-of-resilience).

Dansicker, Jennifer K. "Incredible Teen, Kim Salmeri, Sets an Example of Charity." *Baltimore Sun*, November 28, 2011. Retrieved August 2012 (http://articles.baltimoresun.com/2011-11-28/explore/bs-exha-forest-hill-kim-salmeri-an-incredible-teen-with-a-plan-20111128_1_service-dogs-cpl-canine-partners).

Duckworth, Angela L., et al. "Deliberate Practice Spells Success: Why Grittier Competitors Triumph at the National Spelling Bee." *Social Psychological and Personality Science*, September 6, 2011. Retrieved August 2012 (http://www.sas.upenn.edu/~duckwort/images/Deliberate%20Practice%20Spells%20Success.full.pdf).

Duckworth, A. L, et al. "Grit: Perseverance and Passion for Long-term Goals." National Center for Biotechnology

Information, June 2007. Retrieved August 2012 (http://www.ncbi.nlm.nih.gov/pubmed/17547490).

Glei, Jocelyn K. "The Future of Self-Improvement, Part I: Grit Is More Important Than Talent." 99U.com, 2011. Retrieved August 2012 (http://99u.com/articles/7094/The-Future-of-Self-Improvement-Part-I-Grit-Is-More-Important-Than-Talent).

Greenberg, Chris. "National Spelling Bee Winner: Snigdha Nandipati Wins 2012 Scripps Competition." *Huffington Post*, May 31, 2012. Retrieved August 2012 (http://www.huffingtonpost.com/2012/05/31/national-spelling-bee-winner-2012-snigdha-nandipati_n_1561120.html).

Harris, Beth. "Olympics 2012: Bethesda's Katie Ledecky, 15, Wins 800 Free." *Washingtion Times*, August 3, 2012. Retrieved September 2012 (http://www.washingtontimes.com/news/2012/aug/3/london-olympics-2012-us-15-year-old-katie-ledecky-/?page=all).

Hillard, Gloria. "Blindness Not Enough to Sideline Teen." NPR.org, November 6, 2011. Retrieved September 2012 (http://www.npr.org/2011/11/06/142031957/blindness-not-enough-to-sideline-california-teen?ps=cprs).

Johnson, Avery, and Roy Johnson. *Aspire Higher: Winning On and Off the Court with Determination, Discipline, and Decisions.* New York, NY: HarperCollins, 2008.

Lehrer, Jonah. "Which Traits Predict Success? (The Importance of Grit)." *Wired*, March 14, 2011. Retrieved August 2012 (http://www.wired.com/wiredscience/2011/03/what-is-success-true-grit/).

Mangan, Katherine. "Traits of the 'Get It Done' Personality: Laser Focus, Resilience, and True Grit." *Chronicle of Higher Education*, August 2012. Retrieved September 2012 (http://chronicle.com/article/Traits-of-the-Get-It-Done/133291).

Masterson, Judy. "Waukegan High Valedictorian Has 'Sheer Grit and Determination.'" *Lake County News-Sun*, May 28, 2011. Retrieved August 2012 (http://newssun.suntimes.com/news/5608514-418/valedictorian-has-sheer-grit-and-determination.html).

Peterson, Christopher, and Martin E. P. Seligman. *Character Strengths and Virtues: A Handbook and Classification.* Washington, D.C.: American Psychological Association, 2004.

Tenner, Edward. "Can a New York Day School Teach True Grit?" *Atlantic*, September 16, 2011. Retrieved August 2012 (http://www.theatlantic.com/national/archive/2011/09/can-a-new-york-day-school-teach-true-grit/245139).

# INDEX

## ABOUT THE AUTHOR

Ramona Siddoway is an author from Texas who has also written on the character strength of self-control.

## PHOTO CREDITS

Cover, p. 3 © iStockphoto.com/Scott Hailstone; p. 5 Kimberly Salmeri; pp. 8, 47 © AP Images; p. 10 Aspen Photo/Shutterstock.com; p. 13 Monkey Business Images/ the Agency Collection/Getty Images; p. 15 Sabine Duerichen/LOOK/Getty Images; p. 19 Kelly Cestari/ ASP/CI/Getty Images; p. 20 jstudio/Shutterstock.com; p. 25 Gary S. Chapman/Photographer's Choice RF/Getty Images; p. 27 Jupiterimages/Creatas/Thinkstock; p. 29 Sami Sarkis/Photographer's Choice RF/Getty Images; p. 32 auremar/Shutterstock.com; p. 35 Robin Hauser Reynolds; p. 38 Jordan Siemens/Iconica/Getty Images; p. 41Fabrice Coffrini/AFP/Getty Images; p. 44 Patrick McDermott/Getty Images; p. 45 Redchopsticks/Getty Images; p. 50 Jack Hollingsworth/Photodisc/ Thinkstock; cover, back cover, interior pages background graphic © iStockphoto.com/cajoer.

Designer: Nicole Russo; Photo Researcher: Marty Levick